The world's best
JOKES
for kids
VOLUME 1

The world's best JOKES for kids

VOLUME 1

Every single one illustrated

SWERLING + LAZAR

Andrews McMeel
PUBLISHING®

This book is for

Gabriel + Jamie   Siena + Dash

and all the other
joke-tellers out there,
young and old.

What is heavy and
wears glass slippers?

Cinderelephant.

What did the headteacher say
to the misbehaving egg?

You're egg-spelled!

Which is the most magical dog?

A labracadabrador.

What do you
call a bear with
no ears?

B.

You can tune
a guitar.

But you
can't
tuna fish.

What do you call
a bee that comes
from America?

USB.

Why can't you give
Elsa a balloon?

Because she'll
let it go.

What do you call an elephant that doesn't matter?

An irrelephant.

What did the buffalo say when he dropped his son off at school?

Bison.

What do you call
an ant that won't
go away?

Permanant.

Why was
the king only
12 inches tall?

**Because he was
a ruler.**

How do you describe a person
with no body and just a nose?

Nobody nose.

I was wondering, why does a frisbee appear larger the closer it gets?

Then it hit me.

What do you call the new girl at the bank?

The nutella.

Did you hear about the hungry clock?

It went back four seconds.

**Why do seagulls fly over the sea
and not the bay?**

**Because otherwise
they'd be bagels.**

Why are pirates called pirates?

Because they arrrrrrr.

What do you call having your granny on speed dial?

Instagran.

What happened to the dog that swallowed a firefly?

It barked with de-light!

What treat is never on time?

Choco-late.

What do you call a bear with no teeth?

A gummy bear.

What is E.T. short for?

Because he's got such little legs.

Why did the robber take a bath?

He wanted to
make a clean
getaway.

How do you make an octopus laugh?

With ten-tickles.

What do you call a nervous javelin thrower?

Shakespeare.

Where do crayons go on vacation?

Color-ado.

What do you
call a belt with
a clock on it?

A waist of time.

Why did the
giraffe get
bad grades?

She always had her head
in the clouds.

Have you ever
tried to eat
a clock?

It's very time
consuming.

What did the blanket
say to the bed?

"Don't worry,
I've got you
covered."

What did the one snail
say to the other?

"It's about
slime we started dating."

What do you call a positive bunny?

A hop-timist.

What kind of math do birds like?

Owlgebra.

What do sea monsters eat?

Fish & ships.

**Why did the horse
keep falling over?**

He just wasn't stable.

**Why did the
traffic light
turn red?**

**You would too if you had to
change on the side of the road.**

I've just returned from a once-in-a-lifetime vacation.

Never again.

Why was six scared of seven?

Because seven ate nine.

I hate Russian dolls.

So full of themselves.

What's the best thing about Switzerland?

I don't know, but their flag is a huge plus.

 What did the one fish say to the other?

"Hey, long time no sea."

Why did the tomato blush?

It saw the salad dressing.

What do you
give a horse
with a cold?

Cough
stirrup.

What did Bacon say to Tomato?

"Lettuce get together!"

**Why don't skeletons
fight each other?**

They just don't have the guts.

**What do you call a
line of men waiting
for a haircut?**

A barbeque.

What did the
dad chimney
say to the little
chimney?

"You're too young
to smoke!"

What dog keeps
the best time?

A watch dog.

What did the fish say when
he swam into the wall?

"Dam!"

Why was the dog
feeling sorry for
himself?

Because his life
was so ruff.

What did the girl say when she
threw the slug across the room?

"Gosh,
how slime
flies."

What do you get when you cross a monkey with a peach?

An ape-ricot.

What do you call a polar bear on a desert island?

Lost.

What did Mrs. Earthworm say to her son when he came home late?

"Where on earth have you been?"

What happens
when you annoy
a rabbit?

You have a
bad hare day.

What kind of
lights did Noah
use on the ark?

Flood lights.

Time flies like an arrow.

Fruit flies like a banana.

**What's the best kind of snack to
eat during a horror movie?**

I scream.

**Why was the bed
wearing a disguise?**

Because it was under cover.

Did you hear about the smelly fairy?

Her name was Stinkerbell.

Who brings kittens for Christmas?

Santa claws.

The teacher shouted at me for something I didn't do.

What was it?

My homework.

27

**What did the martian say
to the flower bed?**

**"Take me to
your weeder!"**

**Did you hear about the actress
who fell through the floor?**

**It was just a stage she
was going through.**

When do you stop on green and go on red?

When you're eating watermelon.

Who helped the monster go to the ball?

BALL

Its scary godmother.

Did you hear about the restaurant on Mars?

Great food but no atmosphere.

Why did the girl's parents scream when they saw her grades?

Because she had a bee on her report card.

Why do flamingos stand on one leg?

Because if they lifted it, they'd fall over.

How did the french fry propose to the hamburger?

He gave her an onion ring.

How do you stop a dog from barking in the back seat of the car?

Put him on the front seat of the car.

What do peanut butter and jelly do around the campfire?

They tell toast stories.

What do you get when you cross a pig with a millipede?

Bacon and legs.

What do you call a bear standing in the rain?

A drizzly bear.

What did the mother
corn say to her kids?

"Don't forget
to clean behind
your ears."

What is the craziest way to travel?

By loco-
motive.

Why did the
ninja spend the
day in bed?

He had kung-flu.

Why did the cookie complain about being sick?

He was feeling crummy.

What is a baby's motto?

If at first you don't succeed, cry, cry again.

"You missed school yesterday."

"To tell you the truth, I didn't really miss it."

What happens if you eat yeast and shoe polish?

You'll rise and shine every morning!

What do you call an alligator in a vest?

An investigator.

What do you call a fake noodle?

An Impasta.

Where do rabbits go after their wedding?

On a bunny-moon.

Why did the little birdie fly to the hospital?

To get tweetment.

What is extremely heavy, has 6 wheels, and flies?

A garbage truck.

How did the
snail get a view
of New York
City?

By shell-icopter.

Why did the man jump up and
down before drinking his juice?

The instructions on the carton
said, "Shake well before drinking."

Why did the chicken cross the mobius strip?

To get to the same side.

What did the tree say to the flower?

"I'm rooting for you."

Why did the
man run around
his bed?

Because he was trying to
catch up on his sleep.

Can a flea
jump higher
than a bus?

Of course! Buses can't jump.

Why wouldn't the monster
eat the clown?

Because he suspected it
would taste funny.

Why are ghosts
such bad liars?

Because you can see right
through them.

Why did the
math book look
so sad?

It had lots of
problems.

What did one wall
say to the other?

"Let's meet at the corner."

What does a raincloud wear under its clothes?

Thunderwear.

Why did the banana wear sunscreen on the beach?

He didn't want to peel.

How did the
baseball player
lose his house?

He made his
home run.

Why did the golfer wear
two pairs of pants?

In case he got a hole in one.

Why was everyone
looking up and cheering?

They were
ceiling fans.

Slept like a log
last night.

Woke up in the
fireplace.

What do you call a pig
that knows karate?

A pork chop.

Did you hear about the
claustrophobic astronaut?

He just needed space.

Why was the broom late for school?

Because it over swept.

Why was the nose feeling sad?

Because it was tired of being picked on.

What nursery rhyme do camels like best?

Humpty Dumpty.

What do you call a dentist who
fixes crocodiles' teeth?

Totally crazy.

Did you hear about the teacher
who was cross-eyed?

He couldn't
control his
pupils.

How does an Eskimo fix his broken toys?

With iglue.

Why can one never take balloons seriously?

Because they're full of hot air.

Why couldn't the monster get to sleep?

Because it was afraid that there were children under the bed.

What stays in the corner yet travels across the world?

Ben + Eileen Dover
13 Avocado Avenue
Sydney
Australia

A stamp.

Why didn't the
skeleton go to
the ball?

Because he
had no body
to dance
with.

What's the difference between
boogers and broccoli?

Kids won't eat broccoli.

What did one flea say to the other?

Shall we hop there
or take the dog?

What did the one
tube of glue say to
the other?

"Let's stick
together."

I went to the doctor yesterday
and asked if she could do
anything for wind.

So she gave
me a kite.

Why can't a nose be 12 inches long?

Because it would be a foot.

What do you take before every meal?

You take
your seat.

Why did the scarecrow win a medal?

Because he was outstanding in his field.

What do you get when a chicken lays its eggs on the top of a hill?

Eggrolls.

What did the cucumber say to the vinegar?

"This is a fine pickle you've got us into!"

A chicken crossing the road . . .

is poultry in motion.

It's difficult explaining puns to kleptomaniacs.

They always take things, literally.

Why didn't the girl
trust the ocean?

Because there was something
fishy about it.

What do you call
a dinosaur that's
worried all the
time?

A nervous
Rex.

Why did the girl drop the clock
out the window?

Because she
wanted to see
time fly.

What starts with E, ends with E,
and has only one letter in it?

Envelope.

What is a bat's motto?

Hang in there.

What do you get when you cross a comedian with crochet?

A knit wit.

How do cats end a fight?

They hiss and make up.

What do you call a man who rolls around in leaves?

Russell.

What's black and smells like red paint?

Black paint.

What do you
call a Roman
emperor when
he catches
a cold?

Julius Sneezer.

Where should
you leave your dog
when you go shopping?

In the
barking lot.

What do you give an elephant with big feet?

Lots of space.

What do cats call mice?

Delicious.

Why did the baker stop making donuts?

He got tired of the hole thing.

**What do you get when you cross
a cow with an earthquake?**

A milkshake.

How do you toast a sheep?

**"Here's to
ewe!"**

Why did the computer cross the road?

To get a byte to eat.

What do you call a robot that always takes the longest route?

R2 Detour.

What do you call
a chicken with
lettuce in its eye?

Chicken caesar
salad.

What did the sushi say to the bee?

WASABI!

What has one
horn and gives
milk?

A milk truck.

How did the fisherman go deaf?

He lost his herring.

The worst part about being
a birthday cake is when you're
set on fire...

...and then eaten
by the hero that
saves you.

Why was
the rabbit
unhappy?

She was
having a
bad hare
day.

What gets wetter
as it dries?

A towel.

How do you catch a squirrel?

Climb a tree and act like a nut.

**What did the policemen do
with the hamburger?**

They gave him a good grilling.

**My friend keeps trying to con-
vince me that he's a compulsive
liar.**

But I don't believe him.

Why did the house go to the doctor?

Because it had a window pane.

What happens to astronauts who misbehave?

They're grounded.

On the other hand...

... you have
different fingers.

This is my
step ladder.

I never knew my
biological ladder.

Don't you hate it
when someone
answers their
own questions?

I do.

I, for one, like
Roman numerals.

My wife just found out I replaced
our bed with a trampoline.

She hit the
roof.

I told my doctor that I broke
my arm in two places.

She told me to
stop going to
those places.

Knock Knock.

Who's there?

Knock.

Knock who?

Knock Knock.

Bacon and eggs walk into
a cafe and order some sodas.

**The waiter says, "Sorry,
we don't serve breakfast."**

I really must get rid of
my vacuum cleaner.

It's just
gathering dust.

What do religious rabbits say before they eat?

"Lettuce pray."

Where do you find a cow with no legs?

Right where you left it.

Exaggerations went up by a million percent last year.

How do you count cows?

With a cowculator.

What do you call
a boomerang that
doesn't come back?

A stick.

Two antennas met on a roof,
fell in love, and got married.

**The ceremony was
boring, but the reception
was brilliant.**

What occurs once in a minute, twice in a moment, but never in a decade?

The letter "m."

The grammar teacher
was very logical.

He had a lot of
comma sense.

Did you hear about the really rich rabbit?

He was a millionhare.

Why are hairdressers never late for work?

They know all the short cuts.

What is the color of the wind?

Blew.

Where does a sheep go for a haircut?

To the baaa baaa shop.

How much room is needed for fungi to grow?

As mushroom as possible.

How do you know carrots are good for your eyes?

Have you ever seen a rabbit wearing glasses?

Have you heard
about corduroy
pillows?

They're making
headlines.

Knock knock.

Who's there?

Beats.

Beats who?

Beats me.

What's an elephant's favorite vegetable?

Squash.

Two penguins walk into a bar . . .

which is stupid, because the second one really should have seen it.

Where do cows go for entertainment?

To the moo-vies.

What do you get when you cross a parrot and a centipede?

A walkie-talkie.

Do you want to hear a bad cat joke?

Just kitten.

What is a rabbit's
favorite dance style?

Hip-Hop.

What do you call a ghost's
mom and dad?

Transparents.

What do you call a bear in a phone booth?

Stuck.

What does the man in the moon do when his hair gets too long?

Eclipse it!

What did the grape say
when he was pinched?

Nothing, he
just gave a
little wine.

Did you hear about the vampire
bike that went round biting people?

It was a vicious cycle.

Why was the cookie sad?

Because her mom
was a wafer so long.

Why did the chicken
cross the road?

To hunt somebody down.

Knock knock!

Who's there?

The chicken.

What's the difference between a
weird rabbit and a sporty rabbit?

One's a bit
funny,
the other's
a fit bunny.

What did the cat
say when she lost
all her money?

"I'm paw!"

"This is your captain speaking."

"AND THIS IS
YOUR CAPTAIN
SHOUTING."

What did one plant say to another?

"What's stomata?"

What do you call a cat that lives in an igloo?

An Eskimew.

Where do you find giant snails?

On the ends of giants' fingers.

Yesterday I held the door open for a clown.

I thought it was a nice jester.

You can always
trust a glue
salesman.

They tend to
stick to their
word.

I didn't realize my dad was
a construction site thief.

But when I got home, all
the signs were there.

Can February march?

No, but
April may.

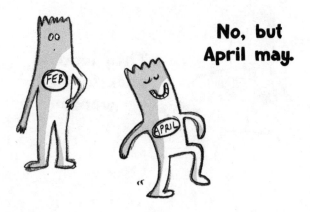

What starts with a P, ends with an E, and has ten thousand letters in it?

A post
office.

I really wanted
a camouflage shirt . . .

but I couldn't find one.

"I stand
corrected,"

. . . said the man in the
orthopedic shoes.

What swims and starts with a T?

Two ducks.

What's orange and sounds like a parrot?

A carrot.

Have I told you the deja vu joke before?

The past, present, and future
walk into a bar.

It was tense.

What did the farmer say when
he couldn't find his tractor?

"Where's my
tractor?"

How many cats can you put
into an empty box?

**Only one. After that,
the box isn't empty.**

I feel sorry for that calendar.

**Its days are
numbered.**

What's brown
and sticky?

A stick.

Why did the two fours skip lunch?

They already 8.

Why did the can crusher quit his job?

Because it was soda pressing.

How much did the pirate pay for his hook and peg?

An arm and a leg.

What do you call
a crocodile with
GPS?

A navi-gator.

How can you drop a raw egg onto
a cement floor without cracking it?

Any way you want.
Cement floors are very hard to crack.

What color is a burp?

Burple.

Why did the toilet paper go downstairs?

To get to the bottom.

What side of a
sheep has the
most wool?

The outside.

What is heavy
forward but not
backward?

Ton.

Did you hear about the two bed
bugs who met in the mattress?

They got married in the spring.

What's the dream of
every cow?

To go to the
mooooo-n.

What's the difference
between roast beef
and pea soup?

You can roast beef, but you
can't pea soup.

How did the dinosaur know we were coming?

The bronto-saw-us.

What accidents happen every 24 hours?

Day breaks

and night falls.

I was struggling to figure out how lightning works.

Then it struck me.

"Nostalgia just isn't what it used to be . . ."

My sister and I often
laugh about how
competitive we are.

But I laugh
more.

How did the
scientist invent bug
spray?

He started
from scratch.

What did the bride say when she dropped her bouquet?

"Whoopsy daisies!"

What did the orange say to the banana when they were looking for the apple?

"Keep your eyes peeled."

What do you call cheese that isn't yours?

Nacho cheese.

How can you go surfing
in the kitchen?

**On the
microwave.**

What do you get when you wake up and
realize you've run out of coffee?

A depresso.

What did the sheep say to his girlfriend?

"I love ewe."

Why did the laptop get glasses?

To improve its web sight.

What was the pessimist's blood type?

B-negative.

Why couldn't the monkey catch the banana?

The banana split.

What did the one leaf say to the other?

"I'm falling for you."

How do you make a hot dog stand?

You take away its chair.

Where does a grumpy gorilla sit?

Anywhere he likes.

Why do giraffes have such long necks?

Because their feet smell.

Which word is always spelled incorrectly?

Incorrectly.

Why did the chicken cross the playground?

To get to the other slide.

What's orange and points north?

A magnetic carrot.

What do you call a dinosaur wearing a blindfold?

A doyouthinkhesaurus?

How do you get down from a camel?

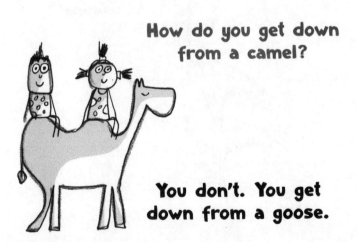

You don't. You get down from a goose.

Did I tell you the gossip
about the butter?

Actually, I don't
think I will, as you'll
probably spread it.

What did the ostrich say
when it laid a square egg?

"Owwww!"

What do you get when you cross
a laptop with an elephant?

Loads of memory.

What do you call a homeless snail?

A slug.

What do you call two giraffes
in a head-on collision?

A giraffic
jam.

How do bananas
answer the phone?

"Yellow."

What snake has the cleanest
front window on its car?

The windshield viper.

How did the calendar survive on
the desert island?

**It ate all the
dates.**

**What do you call spiders
on honeymoon?**

Newlywebs.

**Why was the potato
wearing socks?**

**To keep her
pota-toes warm.**

**What do you
call a lost
wolf?**

A where wolf.

What does a musician use
to clean her teeth?

A tuba toothpaste.

How do monkeys stay fit?

They go to the jungle
gym.

What do you call the soft tissue between a shark's teeth?

A slow swimmer.

She had a photographic memory.

But sadly she never developed it.

Why can't you hear a pterodactyl in the bathroom?

Because it has a silent pee.

The World's Best Jokes for Kids Volume 1

Andrews McMeel Publishing
a division of Andrews McMeel Universal
1130 Walnut Street, Kansas City, Missouri 64106

www.andrewsmcmeel.com

19 20 21 22 23 BVG 10 9 8 7 6 5 4 3 2

ISBN: 978-1-4494-9798-9

Library of Congress Control Number: 2018952722

Made by:
Berryville Graphics
25 Jack Enders Lane
Berryville, VA 22611
2nd printing—September 21, 2019

For lots more funny, silly, and random jokes,
visit us online:
www.lastlemon.com/silliness
www.instagram.com/silliness.is
www.facebook.com/silliness.is

Send us a joke. If we like it,
we'll illustrate it:
www.lastlemon.com/silliness/submit

ATTENTION: SCHOOLS AND BUSINESSES

Andrews McMeel books are available at quantity discounts with
bulk purchase for educational, business, or sales promotional use.
For information, please e-mail the Andrews McMeel Publishing
Special Sales Department: specialsales@amuniversal.com.